Pout-Pout Fish

Pout-Pout Fish Goes to the Dentist

Written by **Wes Adams**   Illustrated by **Isidre Monés**

Based on the *New York Times*–bestselling Pout-Pout Fish books
written by Deborah Diesen and illustrated by Dan Hanna

Farrar Straus Giroux
New York

With thanks to Jeremy Dixon, D.D.S., of Gramercy Pediatric Dentistry, and to Madeline Apfel, D.D.S.

Farrar Straus Giroux Books for Young Readers
An imprint of Macmillan Publishing Group, LLC
120 Broadway, New York, NY 10271

Color separations by Embassy Graphics
Printed in China by RR Donnelley Asia Printing Solutions Ltd., Dongguan City, Guangdong Province
Designed by Aram Kim
First edition, 2020
10 9 8 7 6 5 4 3 2 1

mackids.com

Library of Congress Control Number: 2019948812
ISBN: 978-0-374-31049-3

Our books may be purchased in bulk for promotional, educational, or business use.
Please contact your local bookseller or the Macmillan Corporate and Premium Sales Department at
(800) 221-7945 ext. 5442 or by email at MacmillanSpecialMarkets@macmillan.com.

It was a busy, busy day for Mr. Fish. He had many things on his to-do list, including an appointment to see the dentist.

POST OFFICE
LIBRARY
GREEN MARKET
TOY STORE
DENTIST

P. P.

After mailing letters at the post office, Mr. Fish went
to the library to return a book and check out a few more.
At the circulation desk, he looked up at the clock. His dentist
appointment was in just a few hours.

"I don't think I will have time to see the dentist today," he said to Mr. Eight.

"Keep your appointment," his friend recommended. "Seeing your dentist is important."

At the green market, Mr. Fish saw Miss Shimmer at the sea-sponge stand.

He told her about all the tasks left on his to-do list. "And my dentist appointment is coming up soon!" He thought about it. "Do I even need to go? I brush my teeth almost every day, and I floss when I have time. I doubt my teeth need any cleaning."

"Dentist visits help keep your whole mouth healthy," she said. "Put that appointment at the top of your list!"

At the toy store, Mr. Fish bought a new outfit for Snoozy Snuggly. He saw Ms. Clam, who was shopping for a bicycle helmet. Mr. Fish helped her pick out a sturdy one in her favorite color. Then he realized it was almost time for his dentist visit. "Does a dentist appointment really matter?"

Ms. Clam tapped her helmet. "Yes," she replied. "I may not have teeth like yours, but I know how important it is to take good care of yourself."

Mr. Fish knew his friends were right. It was time to see the dentist!

When he entered the office, the receptionist greeted him warmly. "Welcome, Mr. Fish!"

Soon a dental hygienist showed him to a room and sat him in a big comfy chair. The hygienist put on gloves and a mask.

"The gloves and mask help prevent germs from spreading," he told Mr. Fish.

The hygienist gave Mr. Fish a pair of sunglasses to wear. "The light can be a little bright," he explained. Then he used special tools to gently scrape the surfaces of Mr. Fish's teeth.

"Plaque is a film that builds up on your teeth," he told Mr. Fish. "Bacteria that live in plaque can cause tiny holes in your teeth called cavities. Daily brushing removes plaque, and so does a dental cleaning."

He switched to a different scraping tool. "If plaque stays on too long, it can harden. That's called tartar. I'm removing a bit of that now," he said.

Next, the hygienist used a motorized brush to polish Mr. Fish's teeth. Mr. Fish got to choose which flavor of toothpaste he wanted. "That's an easy choice," he said. "Seaweed flavor!"

"Now we'll take some X-rays," said the hygienist. He put a special vest on Mr. Fish, who opened his mouth and bit down to hold the film trays in place. The hygienist used a camera to take X-ray pictures of the inside of Mr. Fish's teeth.

Finally, it was time for the dentist to come in. "Hello, Mr. Fish!" she said. She examined his mouth and tongue. A tiny mirror helped her get a better view. She counted Mr. Fish's teeth and felt to see if any were wiggling. "When you were little, you had baby teeth," she said. "As you got bigger, those teeth fell out to make room for grown-up teeth to come in." She looked inside his mouth a little more. "Your grown-up teeth all look good to me."

Mr. Fish was glad to hear this.

Then she checked each tooth for cavities. "I don't see any holes in your teeth. But let's take a look at your X-rays."
She examined the pictures.
"Your choppers look good on the inside, too!" she said.
This made Mr. Fish happy.

The dentist asked Mr. Fish about his tooth-brushing routine.
Mr. Fish told her the same thing he had told Miss Shimmer.
"I brush my teeth almost every day, and I floss when I have time."
But he felt a little worried as he spoke. He wasn't sure if this was
the right answer.

"That's a good start, Mr. Fish," the dentist said. "But the best way to keep your teeth healthy is to brush for two minutes, morning and night. Then floss once a day after brushing to clean all the tight spaces between your teeth."

That made sense to Mr. Fish.

"I can do it!" he said.

"Good!" the dentist said. "And treat your teeth to a new brush every three months."

The day had been a busy one, but Mr. Fish had learned a lot.
He was glad he'd gone to the dentist.

He swam home happily. Now he knew everything he needed
to do to keep a great big, healthy . . .

DENTIST